# The Unicornskin Drum

## Stella Bahin

# The Unicornskin Drum

## Stella Bahin

Three Drops Press
Sheffield, England

Three Drops Press
Sheffield, United Kingdom
www.threedropspoetry.co.uk

Three Drops Press is an independent imprint of Endaxi Press.

ISBN 978-1-907375-16-3

Photo © Stella Bahin 2016
Book and cover design © Kate Garrett 2016

*for Simon Gibbons*

Chapter One ...................................................................9

Chapter Two...................................................................19

Chapter Three................................................................23

Chapter Four .................................................................31

Chapter Five ..................................................................37

Chapter Six.....................................................................41

Acknowledgements......................................................54

Other titles from Three Drops Press ........................55

# Chapter One

They say tomorrow never comes, but, whatever they may say, once upon a time always does. Because, there was once a daughter who'd been knitting a blanket since her hands could wield the needles, and this is the truth, for it was told by one who is not to be doubted. They called her The Knitter. The blanket was pearled with vibrant colour against vibrant colour, including The Knitter's own clothes from babyhood, knitted for her by her great-grandmother, carefully unravelled for reuse, and all sorts of other collected woollens and threads.

The Knitter lived with her mother and father in an old house with a porch to the west and an old walled garden to the east and in that walled garden was an even older well. Every day, while the father was out working, the villagers would arrive, in turn, with pails to be filled with water. And the mother, with a light and cheery step, would carry the pails through the house to the well and back to the porch while The Knitter sat knitting the colourful blanket for one day when she'd be as happily wed as her parents.

Although she'd no sweetheart, as yet, she imagined her blanket spread in a big room on her own big marital bed, with her, and her husband, happy and cosy, side by side, beneath its colourful patterns.

One evening The Knitter waited for her father's return with particular excitement for she'd completely knitted the blanket, and, meanwhile, freed from her needles at last, she wished to invite the villagers inside the house to keep company with her: *Why must our visitors wait in the porch while you fetch the water, Mother?* she asked.

*Because the water's for all, Daughter, but the house, garden, and well, they belong to us,* the mother replied. This was her way and the way of all well-keepers previous.

When the father returned and had greeted his wife, The Knitter showed him her work. He was greatly pleased and told her they'd take it to a far away market where they might glean a good price for it. She would've protested that she'd made the blanket for her husband to-be, not he, her father, but he had already taken it, it was done, and she respected him, so she did not protest.

*You're no longer a child, Daughter,* he told her. *And you must stay here and well-keep.*

The Knitter felt the top of her head looking down at herself in her long frock and laced boots, smaller than her parents, but yes, full grown. She looked at her hands, empty of knitting, then at her father's hands, folding the blanket. She looked at the home she'd lived in lifelong, her eyes resting on the familiar white apron doubled round her mother's waist, sighing. Then she looked through the window at the clouds impelled south across the blue by the north wind, and sighed again.

She neither wished her parents to leave with her taken blanket nor to well-keep, but when the day came for her parents to set off with the horse and cart she waved them farewell without tears, thinking, "I'm no longer a child, indeed." And, with her mother's apron firmly doubled round her waist she repeated: *The water's for all, but the house, garden, and well, belong to us,* to every villager who requested to step beyond the porch in her parents' absence. *They may return any moment,* she added, peering hopefully up the pathway, letting nobody in.

One windy evening, a messenger arrived. He told The Knitter her parents had been murdered by thieves and returned the blanket to her, which was all that remained.

"Only this?" she thought when the messenger had left, squeezing the blanket to her as if it might embrace her or tell her otherwise. It did neither. She held it, with all her hopes knitted into it, at arm's length, bright as ever leaving her to answer the question: "What am I to make of it, that my parents are dead and gone?" by herself.

Day after sorrowful day, week after sorrowful week, no answer came. She couldn't bear to see the blanket, which knew nothing of sorrow with its cheery colours, and stuffed it away along with all her colourful frocks too, dressing herself in her great-grandmother's widow's clothes that fitted her neatly instead.

When the villagers came kindly for their water, The Knitter couldn't even smile for them then. It was all she could do to turn the well-handle, tip the well-bucket, and drag their filled pails back to the porch for them under the weight of the sorrow she now bore. When a young farmhand invited The Knitter to come with him to listen to a singer who was to be visiting the village green, she refused. The village was far too far for one so grief-burdened.

Come evening, the wind brought the *thud-thudding* of a drum to her ears and she cried into her pillow for her lost father but was no lighter for that shedding.

The next year, when the farmhand sent his sister to invite The Knitter to listen to The Singer on the green, she refused again. Come evening, she opened the window of her small bedroom to deliberately hear the *thud-thudding* of the drum and cried onto the sill for her lost mother, but still grew no lighter.

The following year, when that sister sent her aunt to invite The Knitter to the green, The Knitter refused once more. But, come evening, she stepped, with her sorrow-heavy feet, into the garden and leant against the well to hear The Singer's drum. There she cried for herself, The Knitter, her tears falling into the well-water to the rhythm of the distant *thud-thudding* with a *plink-plink*.

The year after that, nobody invited The Knitter to the green, and by the time she heard the evening owl, *oo oo oo, oo oo oo*, she thought no one would. But an elderly crone arrived at her door with a crimson shawl over her straggly-haired head and three teeth the colour of dandelions in her mouth, saying she wished to go hear The Singer but had no companion. The Knitter saw that this shrivelled elder, bent over a gnarly stick, held in gnarly hands, carried far weightier sorrows than she, yet with far greater composure.

*Call me Esther*, said the crone.

The Knitter was taken aback to hear a name used so lightly!

Esther smiled looking down steadily into The Knitter's eyes, as if, even though they'd never met, they were already in a friendship.

*Hello Esther*, greeted The Knitter, nodding politely.

*Have you something bright to wear, fit for a festive outing?* asked Esther from under her crimson shawl, while a scent emanated from her like the scent of the amber pine as she eyed The Knitter's dark mourning clothes.

The Knitter remembered the blanket she'd made and told Esther of it who wrapped it round The Knitter like a cape. Seeing its vivid threads and feeling its warmth about her, The Knitter agreed to come listen to The Singer on the green with Esther, and the old woman and the young set off together apace, slow and steady, arm in arm.

Once they were scuffling through a cacophonous, jostling crowd, The Knitter thought she'd made a mistake, but then they were at the front, and there, on a platform, under a canopy held up by poles wreathed with red ivy and black roses, was The Singer, and their eyes met with a twinkle such as her parents had twinkled between themselves and none other.

*Fine cape*, he commented as they passed to find a patch of grass on which to sit, glancing up and down at the blanket she'd made for when she'd be married.

*Thank you.* The Knitter replied, looking to where they were heading, away, her head bowed, yet still seeing all his details bright as torchlight in her mind: his black hair to his shoulders, his one-pronged black goatee pointing up; his loose white top, open as a nightshirt; his red trousers, full as ladies' bloomers; the nude-leather slippers on his feet, a second flesh; his deep grey bowler hat on his head with two swan quills, proud as a pair of horns, piercing from its gleaming silver band; and the round belly silver skin drum between his knees; how he was perched on purple and aqua cushions made of silk on a small three-legged pine seat, with a brown- and white-freckled hawk at his side that had noticed her also. The Knitter listened, eyes averted, as The Singer began *thud-thudding* his drum, in vibrant close-up, till he added a sound that was his singing voice when she not only looked up at him but stood up to find herself dancing along with the many.

Hours flew as the crow to the music becoming done, lulling The Knitter ready to stay for the hog roast and punch laced with rum next, hoping to happen speak with him, but then her companion, Esther, happened gossip her first that The Singer was about to be married. *To be married?* echoed The Knitter as if she'd misheard, though she'd heard Esther's words head to toe and through and through precisely.

Esther smiled at the deepened pink in The Knitter's cheeks proving to Esther there was no need for Esther to go spelling it out again to this flush-faced woman who was now peering up at The Singer and the hawk on his shoulder and the drum under his arm as if he had struck her, while he acknowledged the congratulatory villagers as contentedly as if the world were a perfect treat arranged for his delectation, till he spotted The Knitter, watching him, when his face lit brighter still as if to say, *all this before me, and now you, the iced cake of it!* and immediately headed for her, his eyes twinkling as they'd twinkled throughout the evening. The eye-sparks made The Knitter jump! *I must leave!* she hissed at Esther as this to-be-married gentleman fast approached her through the crowd.

*Speak with him,* Esther urged her, yet The Knitter shook her head dumbly. He was near.

*You're fit to walk home, aren't you, Esther?* The Knitter enquired, backing away, dreading an answer that would mean she would have to tarry a moment longer, wanting to run from him as if for her life.

*I'll walk Esther home.* said The Singer, taking Esther's arm. Arrived.

*Thank you, Yendle.* replied Esther, simply, placing a hand on top of his, and The Knitter reddened darker to be faced with these two intimacies at once: the spoken exchange of names, and a physical contact by him she would've relished for herself. After uttering quick polite partings, she then ran the miles home to her house, chanting:

*She knows him, she knows him... I know his name, I know his name...* under her breath, not daring to voice that name which had only been overheard, not offered directly by him for her use, and she knew, by custom, that it would be as a theft to use it.

That night she dreamt she and The Singer were running laughing across a field lush with blades of grass to a place neither of them had ever been to the *thud-thudding* of his beautiful silvery drum with the hawk looping the air between them. When she woke she could still hear the *thud-thudding* since her heartbeat was loudly carrying it on, and then there was the door too, knocking. She ran to it wondering who it might be so soon after dawn and it was The Singer with his hawk, a pair of empty pails, and his drum. He wished to deliver water to the inn he'd slept in as a thank you to his hosts.

*Did I wake you?* he asked with a smile. *Though you answered your door in a trice, that's surely your nightdress.*

The Knitter looked at herself in astonishment. She'd given no thought to either her attire or bare feet. She lifted one foot, then the other: they were light! And hadn't she danced the night long and run the way home and sped to the door just now to open it?

The Singer watched her with raised eyebrows, waiting for a reply, and the hawk simply watched. Seeing The Singer's preparedness for listening, she entrusted him with the story of the weight of her sadness and how she'd come by it through her parents' murders, and, to her surprise, was now freed of it. As she spoke, a chilly breeze from the west pressed the thin white fabric of her nightdress to her shape, but The Singer's soothing gaze kept her warm and unashamed.

*Thank you,* said The Singer once she'd spoken her tale, handing her the big pails.

Whilst remembering her mother's rules, *the water's for all, but the house, garden, and well, they belong to us...* The Knitter, with the thrill and tremble of rebellion, disobeyed them: *Won't you come in?*

The Singer nodded, but remained yet in the porch, so The Knitter left the doors wide in case his slippers might be called to follow in the direction of the point of his chin, like his hawk, which flew directly behind her, through the building, and past her, to land high on the well's slate roof. The Knitter stared from house to hawk to house in a giddiness of hoping The Singer would come through, making her forgetful. The hawk cocked its head at the well-handle and The Knitter thanked the hawk for reminding her of her purpose and turned it. It turned so readily The Knitter wondered if she'd drawn the well-bucket empty, but it brimmed. Lifting and pouring the bucket to fill the pails and shifting them came easily too. She laughed with a gurgle like tipping water to then find, while bearing two full pails, that her feet were lighter than even her mother's had been!

She placed the pails happily at The Singer's feet, though he had remained outside, in the porch, for he was still there! Noticing as she did so that he smelt like the mouth-watering marzipan for eating only on The Festival Day, but deeper in tone, and more musk; marzipan gossiped to be painted with pure gold at The Palace on every grand occasion. The hawk settled back on The Singer's shoulder as he politely thanked her.

*Are you the author of your songs?* she enquired of him, open-faced with admiration, since he seemed in no heat to depart.

*No. I'm the chooser of them,* he replied with his chin high, and smiling, but The Knitter knew a sorrow when she saw one and figured that there were songs of his own locked within him that he only yearned to sing.

*Well, you sing and drum those chosen songs, authored by others, beautifully,* she crooned with a croak in her throat though withholding his name, "Yendle", from the tip of her tongue.

The hawk looked at her mouth, opening and closing its beak as if wishing to speak it for her: *Yendle.*

The Singer thanked The Knitter graciously: *I'm flattered.* As he did so, a ray of sunlight painted pure gold the bare of his neck, ordering her to reach up on tiptoes and touch; an order which taboo scolded her for even attending. She trembled, confused. The hawk flapped its wings, opening wider its sharp beak.

*Would you care for some breakfast?* she offered The Singer, urgently, her heart *thud-thudding.*

The Singer nodded as the hawk listened from his shoulder to her breast, as if hearing the beat.

The Knitter stepped aside for The Singer to enter the house. He did not move.

*I've a sweetheart,* The Singer told her, keeping to the porch, disgracing her *thud-thudding* heart which, so near to his own, had quite forgotten that he was a to-be-married gentleman.

"Would I were your sweetheart," she thought, and the hawk looked at her eyes, as if reading an open book, her unlocked private diary, every word, every pressed flower, every memento, every sketch. The Knitter smiled at the hawk, spreading her hands towards it, shrugging her shoulders, at ease with its seeking eyes, harbouring nothing.

*We're building a house, with a garden...* The Singer added.

"I have a house, and a garden," she thought, and the hawk eyed her up and down, as if taking her size.

*...and once it's built, we'll be married. We intend a large family,* The Singer continued.

"Would I were your wife," thought The Knitter, placing her hands upon her belly and thinking of she and The Singer cosy and happy under her colourful blanket. The hawk dipped its head towards her placed hands.

The Singer noted the gesture of her hands too, and nodded, which she took as a cue for her to speak.

*Then farewell,* she said with genuine warmth, only belied by her heart *thud-thudding*: "Stay! Stay!"

The hawk cried out as if in answer, making her start, and The Singer blinked the hawk to immediately close its beak. The Knitter's heart calmed the same moment. The Singer then placed his drum at her feet, explaining, *I need both hands for the water,* then stared at her like a co-actor in a play, hoping she would remember her lines before he had to prompt her.

*I'll tend it for you,* she quoted uncertainly, not knowing from where the words came.

With a final nod and a grin so delightful her mirroring of it made them both, momentarily, nothing but grin, The Singer picked up the pails and left, the tin of them gleaming like sterling and the water glistening like liquid gems as the hawk took flight on ahead. And the sight of his departure inspired a poignancy more intense in The Knitter than she'd thought possible for any creature on earth to experience, let alone she; and with gratitude at having felt, and survived such a feeling, she became more buoyant from that instant than ever in her life.

*I'll tend it,* she repeated her own words, to tease herself, giggling, as she placed his drum by the hearth and lit the day's fire, for surely: *he'll return for it soon and I'll ask him to fetch it from the hearth for himself to ensure he comes in!* she said, trusting his leaving of the drum spoke words beneath the ones he'd voiced, forgetting, again, that he was to be married.

Fearful that smuts would spoil the drum's pale skin, she covered it with her blanket before taking the dark mourning clothes and tossing them on top of the flames. She dressed herself in a pretty frock she'd not worn since her orphaning and flitted about her work from door to well to door, confident of The Singer's return, till the thirteenth caller told her he'd left the village directly after delivering the water to the inn.

Throbbing with regret at having burned the mourning clothes, she slumped, slowly, into the fireside armchair. "The man who confirms my heartbeat to my heart, my sight to my eyes and my step to my feet has a sweetheart," she considered. "The man who's restored my delight in my blanket is building a house with a garden for that sweetheart to become his wife." Her sorrow returned, more weightily. She became still in the chair, barely breathing.

With nightfall, a blast of wind whooshed down the chimney, chilling, but not shifting her to even a shivering. Rather, she was pleased by the straightforward cooling of her skin that had flushed so irrationally in The Singer's presence; flushed as if her impulsive heat should matter to her and might matter to him. The next blast came colder and more forceful, spattering fragments of the firewood beyond the hearth. She didn't move. She might even have ignored the third, noisiest, iciest blast yet, afterwards, but a strange silvery light followed it, glowing through her closed eyelids, a light so weird every hair on her body pricked up.

The Knitter leapt off the chair and onto her feet like a thunderclap. In a moment of unearthly fear, she saw the full moon afloat in her dark room. Her eyes straining, her heart *thud-thudding*, she thought, "I've finally died of heartbreak," before realising she was looking at The Singer's drum from which the wind had blown her blanket. She saw windblown embers smouldering the hearthrug and beat them out, shuddering to think of the drum in flames had its light not shone her awake.

She rebuilt the fire, wrapped herself in her blanket to thaw and sat on the rug blinking at the finely-wrought object left in her custody. Its skin glistened silver in the firelight like his neck gold in the early morning sun.

*May I touch?* she whispered as she reached towards it. Of its own accord, it made a sound: *Thud*. She jumped. Or was it her heart? It made another, louder: *Thud!* It was both.

The skin felt taut and soft. Her palms and finger-pads stroked in tender circles every place his hands had touched: the gut ties, the level head and the carved wooden belly, swollen as a belly soon to birth. She could feel his hands beneath her own, crafting the drum, holding it, playing it. She smiled, feeling his hands until his hands were as her own and hers his. She knew, again, for certain: he couldn't forsake this. Comforted, she withdrew her hands. And whatever it was that made it so, was pleased to find her hands remained not quite her own. She covered the drum with her blanket and took herself off up to bed.

# Chapter Two

She woke in the dark with a faint silvery ringing in her head. She blinked sleepily, snuggling back under the covers, vaguely wondering if she were sickening for a fever. There was a *thud* from downstairs matched within her breast.

"The drum?" she wondered, sleepily.

*Thud, thud.*

"How am I to sleep?" she thought.

*Thud!*

The Knitter leapt from her little bed, the ringing loud between her ears. She walked quickly down the stairs towards the drum, fearlessly, well led. In hand. The drum shimmered through the blanket illuminating the room iridescent. She threw the blanket off and spread her hands, energetic with the tug and press of his, directly upon it. A bright image flashed into her mind of a unicorn, rearing, bleeding. She snatched back her hands, knowing at once the skin.

*Did The Singer slay you, unicorn?* The Knitter asked the drum. The drum gleamed, not revealing the answer. *Oh, precious drum*, she said, and carried it upstairs, not wanting others to see this illicit object she was harbouring through her door, or window, and perhaps steal in and handle it and learn of it also. Her room seemed too small for such an object so she entered her parents' room instead, placed the drum at the bedside, climbed up into their large bed, and fell into a sound sleep and dreamed of a gold-leafed glade.

Over the following days and weeks, The Knitter became the talk of the village: she, out of her sad rags and back into glad; she, her service so speedy and cheery; she, with the return of her smiles and laughter; she, with an intriguing glow about her. The villagers invited her to dances and suppers but she stayed put, inside her house, with the unicornskin drum, and no matter how they wheedled from the porch for her to speak more than of the weather or the well-water, she made no mention of the drum or the story it was revealing while she caressed it,

19

or while she slept by it; touch by touch, insight by insight, dream by dream.

The Singer had been a singer even as a gurgling baby, singing of all he perceived: his mother's smile, sunlight on his toes, the blue of the sky, the flavours and warms of milk, singing both of all and to all, life running through him like a rain-fat brook. His father, though he smiled at the boy as if proud, wished him to hold death in his heart and be a poacher, like he, and envied the infant his flowing joy, voiced. The father waited for his son to grow. Every birthday the father handed the boy his long-handled knife till the day the boy could wield it. He then trespassed the boy into the forest that belonged to The King.

The boy didn't know what his father hunted till, in a glade circled by tall trees with golden leaves, he spied the unicorn, at once the most wonderful and terrible thing he'd ever beheld, with his father, his face the face of a stranger, approaching downwind, knife up.

*Flee!* the boy tried to shout, even while sensing his father's purpose might then be spat upon himself. But the boy was mute, fixed to the spot with horror till the unicorn was stabbed in its silvery breast: the unicorn, rearing and kicking in self-defence; the man, falling dead, speared by his own knife; the unicorn dropping to lie shivery beside the body. The boy stroked its mane, looking into its eyes.

*Make good come of this,* said the unicorn's eyes, as it died.

The boy neither knew the rogues who might purchase the unicorn's invaluable horn nor how financial fortune could make amends, so took the unicorn's skin. He buried his father in one hand-dug pit and the unicorn, with its precious horn, in the other. Since speaking of this would've both betrayed his family and earned him a hanging for his part, he vowed silence. He left the knife, wrapped in his father's shirt, on his mother's doorstep for the blood to tell her, *nevermore expect him*, then, with the unicornskin bundled, reversed, on his back, began a life of exile.

After days of walking, he came across a minstrel who was on his way overseas to buy a drum. He listened with an attentive heart to the minstrel's numbers. At the minstrel's next stop the boy sang along in duet. The minstrel was enchanted by the boy's song-knowledge, voice, and by the size of the crowd their impromptu performance drew. Once they'd finished, the minstrel was even more pleased with the rewards in coins, ale, and offers of board; greater than he'd previously achieved in a month.

*Who are you and where do you come from, young man?* asked the minstrel.

*Please, call me The Singer. Where I came from, I can't say. I only wish to travel to the drum-makers' with you, with the silver deerskin I carry upon my back,* he replied. *I'd be pleased to sing with you along the way, for my supper, plus my fare across the ocean.*

*The Singer, indeed? Well, Singer, a deal! Why, I'll be The Minstrel then, how's that? Have some ale, we'll drink to it!* The Minstrel agreed.

But by the time they'd reached their destination, The Minstrel wanted to keep The Singer along with the revenue he gleaned in: *You're a boy,* he said, *under my wing. Supposing I was to ask questions about you, back near where you and I picked up? Reckon you were on the run. Keep going with me or I shall.*

So The Singer asked the drum-makers, who were a husband and wife, if they'd buy him from The Minstrel as an apprentice, instead, which cost he'd stay and work off until he'd repaid it. Having seen and heard the boy sing, they said, *Yes!* at once. And after bargaining a high price with them, The Minstrel removed his threat and went on his way, pouch bulging, letting The Singer stay.

Within a few years, The Singer had grown into a young man who'd learned both the language of the land and to outstrip his masters' skills in drum-making. With his drums selling for such high prices, he felt sure the many drums he'd made were enough, by now, to have settled the debt. But keener than ever to keep him, the drum-makers added interest to the sum owed and put up his rent, forcing him to continue singing for them and drum-making, dawn to dusk. Since the day he'd dug the graves, The Singer could no longer sing of what he saw and what he felt, but sang the songs, translated by him into their own language, that he'd learned from the minstrel, as and when his masters bade him. He began to continue working in an old disused barn on their land while they slept, his only companion a hawk.

One morning, The Singer revealed the vast stock of fine drums he'd made at night, proving his indebtedness was spent. There was nothing more they could do than say goodbye. He left with the drum he'd built last, in a new style, the style of his own choosing; a round-bellied drum; the drum that was the reason he'd joined with The Minstrel to travel to the drum-makers' to learn how; and the hawk flew after him; the drum which now sparkled on The Knitter's lap, cherished by her more deeply than she could ever have imagined when promising The Singer she would tend it so many months ago.

# Chapter Three

The more The Knitter had learned of its story; his story; the more she'd felt the essence of him in her body. First it was no longer her hands that weren't quite her own, but her arms too. Then the rest of her body, head over heels, so, as she turned the well-handle or poured the water, The Singer turned or poured along; as she passed words with the villagers, The Singer spoke with her; till, at the close of one evening, she felt his beard pointing invisibly from her own feminine little chin and her sense of his being, within her own, was total. The silvery ringing in her head was strong. Guided by it, and him, in her person, and the house, with its creaking and cracking, she fetched the colourful blanket she'd knitted for the day of her wedding, carried it to the room that once was her parents', now hers, and lay it on the bed.

As The Knitter settled under the covers, the ringing sound purified into a beautiful voice: The Singer, now whole, clearly singing: *The drum is borrowed, your eyes are blue, the bed is old, the night is new...*

*Yendle!* she whispered, enraptured.

He didn't keep within her after that. She woke in the morning to find the bed warm and marzipan-musky at her side. Though alone, he'd lain with her, as man with wife. She stroked the feel of whiskers about her smiling lips, restored to within, thinking: "Today's the day for sure he'll arrive in very person to knock upon my door." She bathed in water infused with lavender fresh-picked from her garden, brushed her hair to a shine leaving it loose over her shoulders, and dressed in a frock boldly patterned with drupes, butterflies, and buds.

The knock came. Her heart *thud-thudding,* she opened the door. It was a young man from the village with a pail in his hand who gawped at her crying, *You look radiant, aglow! Will you walk out with me?*

The Knitter knew if she'd replied straight away, she would've yelled: *The Singer, not you!* so made him wait while she filled his pail, gathering herself.

*No thank you,* she managed to squeeze through gritted teeth as she handed the youth his water. He left looking more captivated than rejected and she banged the door behind him. She slumped against the door, closed, weak with thwarted hope. The wood dug solid into the pliable flesh of her cheek as if admonishing her to face facts she was too soft to accept: the weight and the sorrow. She sprang away, glaring.

*What do you know, door?!* she bellowed, wishing to smash it to smithereens with the heaviest mallet. *I'll give you weight, mighty I will!*

Crash!

The sound came from the outhouse.

*That's probably the mallet now, jumping to it!* The Knitter threatened the door, laughing, and left for the garden to see what had caused the din. She peered at the tools stored neatly in their wooden racks. All seemed orderly, and she turned away, wondering if her ears had misdirected her, when The Singer directed her head to glance down.

The heaviest mallet had fallen to the floor. She now noticed and inspected its empty place on the wall. The nails had turned downwards in the frame that had held it, pointing. *Pick it up,* said The Singer in her mind.

She picked up the mallet by its solid handle and wandered, trance-like, back into the garden, uttering a word she'd only heard once, used by her father when he'd stubbed his toe on the hearthstone. She flinched, looking around guiltily. Nothing happened. She repeated the word louder, remembering how her mother had gasped, frowning at her father, reminding him of *little ears,* too late. She smiled. Looked at the mallet again. Now shouted the swearword...

A pair of wood pigeons took off, startled, from the wall behind the well. The Knitter walked towards it, its ancient stone cut and set by ancestors unknown, bright with sunlight through a split between rainclouds.

*Here?* asked The Knitter, squinting up at the light-shape between the clouds, a defined Y, facing her upright. "Y for yes? Y for Yendle?" she puzzled uncertainly, blinking the Y over the wall, briefly imprinted upon her retina. "This wall, that's been here forever? Because the mallet happened to fall while I was thinking of it and the sky happened to send a Y-shaft of light?!"

*Do it,* insisted The Singer, in her mind.

*Ooh,* she squealed, startled, her heart *thud-thudding.*

*Yes, Yendle!* she cried, swinging the mallet down upon the stone of it, her strength combined with his, *crunch!* understanding what for, on impact.

*Oh, YES!* she repeated, taking another swing, then another, then another, in the rhythm of a drummer drum-drumming.

She, The Knitter, a woman, *thunk-thunking* like a mill.

Before long the villagers, clutching empty pails, had grouped in gossiping huddles beyond the garden, a distance from her. She ignored them and they knew better than to interrupt her.

Once she'd bashed a good gap and cleared a pathway's-worth of rubble she announced:

*Fetch your own water from now on, please, and no more knocking at my door*, and promptly strutted to the shack to dump the mallet before returning to the house, scraping her damp dusty hair from her forehead.

Back inside, she informed the front door: *Next time you knock, it'll be Yendle. Yes, I say it aloud: Yendle...*

*Tap, tap, tap,* the door replied.

The Knitter brushed herself down, heart *thud-thudding.* "Please let it be you," she prayed, opening the door. There in the porch perched his hawk. She looked about excitedly for its master before saying: *You're alone, aren't you?* The hawk blinked at her then flew to perch on the gate. She stepped towards it. The hawk blinked at her then flew to a tree on the lane. *Wait!* she called, understanding it was here to take her to him. *Let me get a coat and lock up!*

Attempting to be as quick as she could she fumbled her buttons and dropped her key, fearing the hawk would vanish, but it had returned to the gate and waited patiently. *Is it far away?* she asked, balking in the porch, remembering the market her parents had never returned from

25

had been *far away*. The hawk flew towards the horizon till out of sight then returned. *I see,* said The Knitter nervously. *Will you stay with me?*

The hawk met her eye, steady, in answer.

*Trust,* whispered The Singer in her mind.

The Knitter drew deep one last breath of home air and stepped on to follow. She followed until dark and beyond, the hawk circling close by. At last, The Knitter heard a distant *thud-thudding* she recognised at once as the sound of The Singer's drumming. "Another drum!" she told herself, faltering. The hawk swooped around her head, and she continued, reassured: "His hawk is with me alone."

Within a field's worth of further walking, she spied the small house with a single light from where the drumming was coming, and exhausted as she was, began running towards the front door. The hawk landed on the gate-latch ahead of her, barring her way and when she reached there, cocked its head towards the lit window.

*Sh.* commanded The Singer, and The Knitter crept towards the window stealthy as a thief to pull herself up by its ledge to peer inside. For a moment she was overjoyed to see him there, at last, in firelight, on cushions, with a distinctively full-bellied drum between his knees, as if returned to her village green, but, in less than a blink, realised her hopeful eyes had duped her. It was a young woman, an expression on her face the like of which The Knitter had not seen before, and she dropped herself from the sight back down to the turf.

*His intended?* she whispered, painfully, to the hawk.

The hawk stared back, unblinking.

*Not she?* she asked, her forehead shadowed with creases, her brow with a frown, her mouth and chin, tugging down.

The hawk blinked.

*Oooh.* she breathed, winded, hanging her head.

The hawk waited for her to be ready to skulk her way out of the garden. Soon as she was free, she ran the way they'd come, stumbling the field's clods till she fell. The hawk landed beside her.

*You brought me here just to show me he receives additional devotion to my own?!* she screamed, panting. The hawk took to the air. The Knitter fought to her feet. *You mean to torture me?!* The hawk flew higher. The Knitter grew louder. *Well, you succeed!* The hawk was gone.

*I'm sorry!* she called into the dark, her frustration replaced by shame at her outburst... *So sorry I frightened you!*

*What've I done?* she whimpered.

Too late, she couldn't withdraw it. She was lost and alone, but for The Singer, inside her.

She placed her hands upon her breast and closed her eyes. *Can you forgive me?* she whispered. A sharp internal smarting was her answer. She'd wronged him, dreadfully. *Please forgive me,* she implored, gulping.

She opened her eyes and peered, terrified, into the night, but without pity for herself, she'd shown none for the hawk. An owl cry, *OO OO OO! OO OO OO!* made her jump. She looked towards the sound. A bat soared, a shadow in flight. Should she follow its direction, she asked herself? The Singer urged her to, sternly, from within.

*Oh, thank you!* she replied, weeping with gratitude: he was yet prepared to help her. She wiped her eyes and took a step, then re-stopped, realising she'd been following clues such as this since the first *thud-thudding* of his drum, when she'd wept tears that needed weeping for her father. What was her choice otherwise, she wondered, peering around? Only one way was right for her and always had been, she knew. Stumbling with fatigue, but allowing herself a grateful smile, she walked on.

She arrived at a track in a forest. Moonlight now rolled out her carpet, and then, at a fork, the familiar *thud-thudding* of a drum took charge of her route. She approached The Singer cautiously. He sat in a clearing with his back to her by a bonfire in a full-length coat of dark leather, with the drum between his knees, intent on rhythm. He stopped suddenly, and she gasped to think she'd disturbed his playing. He stood, gigantic. She backed into the shadows: it wasn't The Singer but another man, with another Singer-made drum. The man moved out of the firelight and into the twiggy blacks and greys with the drum, returning without it, taking one stick from the fire for a torch.

*Follow.*

The Knitter heard The Singer's voice in her head loud as the owl.

"No, I don't want to follow that large man, only you," she replied in her thoughts, disconsolately, and immediately The Singer was silent. She understood, the choice remained hers. The man was leaving. She looked about at the moonlit branches, heard the rustlings of wind and night animals, and reasoned that since it was she who'd scared off the hawk, it was her fault an unwitting stranger was now her only guide, and raced after the man fast as her aching legs and feet would convey her without racket. Holding far back as she could in sight of the flame, it vanished. She picked her way, almost blind, through roots and mud to find it in vain, when it reappeared from behind a tree high in front of her.

*Hello. Rare to find such a little lady, not least alone, in the forest, at night!* said the burly man, expressing the words *little lady* in a manner suggesting she may not fully be a lady.

*I'm lost, I was... walking...* she explained, careful to be truthful, since to tell an inaccuracy gave her heartburn, so it was.

*From where, walking, might I ask?* he said.

She told him and he whistled, *That's some walking!* He poked the flame end of his stick down towards her face and grinned. *Young and comely for a witch, aren't you, little one. Still. Happen we were all young once...*

*I'm no witch!* she protested, laughing, but as she said it, a silvery vibration ran over her body as if her flesh were drum-bound unicornskin and she felt a burn in her throat.

*What did you see then, pray tell?* he asked.

*This...* she replied, pointing.

He waved the flame lofty and laughed. *You're after my stick?!*

*No,* she cried, *I was following the light, your light, I'm lost I say!*

28

The man looked at her face, then past her, in the direction of the fire, then back. She saw his teeth and trembled, was he smiling or grimacing? She knew he was thinking of his drum. "Should I trust him, as your friend, since he has one of your drums? Admit I heard him play, saw him stash the drum away, and am looking for you, its maker?" The Knitter asked The Singer.

*Your question, as questions often do, carries the answer,* The Singer replied to her, thus: "The drum's the man's secret for him alone to spring or keep..." thought The Knitter and The Singer in unison.

As the man looked up the path again, about to speak, The Knitter lurched towards him with big eyes up at him as if begging his sanctuary from whatever he'd seen behind them.

The man touched her shoulder protectively, reassured. *Nothing for you to fear. Walk with me to the lane,* he said. *I'll point you the right direction. You'll need to take board tonight though, it's late, and many an hour to your village.*

Hearing the kindness in his voice, she opened her mouth to confess at least that she'd set off without coin, crust, or beverage...

*NO,* directed The Singer in her thoughts.

And The Knitter kept quiet, silently thanking The Singer, understanding the folly of speaking about personal matters to this stranger.

*Call me Isaac,* said the man, holding a low branch out of her way so she might pass unscratched.

"I must be far from home indeed; we don't give our names so lightly where I'm from..." The Knitter thought to say.

*He knows this, don't speak,* The Singer conducted, and she remained silent, merely nodding at the man as she passed, for holding the branch.

When they reached the lane Isaac said: *Your village lies that way; my house, this,* with a wink.

Whilst The Knitter was wondering whether to return the wink, giggle, or quip, The Singer turned her from Isaac by the shoulders commanding her: *Walk!*

"But I've nothing to steal!" argued The Knitter in her mind, whilst walking, as bidden, straight ahead. "Surely I can at least raise my hand, farewell?"

The Singer answered her with a memory of their night under her knitting.

She didn't turn. She didn't wave.

"Thank you Yendle, I understand," she thought, shuddering, suddenly aware of Isaac's eyes upon her back, humbled to be so unworldly in The Singer's comparison and witness; relieved, once she finally heard the *clomp, clomp,* of Isaac's departing.

# Chapter Four

Soon she had no strength to walk further and was ready to fall. The Singer veined her with threads to keep her upright and blew her like a leaf to a place she might rest: a hedge, by the side of the lane. There she scrabbled till she was safely concealed beneath, when she curled into a tight ball of their oneness and slept until the dawn.

Days later, she shuffled towards her own village at last, in a rainstorm, bony with starvation, mud-stained, ragged and drenched. The boom of the thunder and spangle of the lightning fed the veins The Singer had sewn in her, spinning her on for the hardest mile before home. From place to place she'd heard Singer-made drum after Singer-made drum yet not one of the drummers had been him. But now, here was his hawk perched, bedraggled, on her wall. She looked to the lane, she looked to her porch, confirming, the hawk, once more, was alone.

*Your leg's bandaged, are you hurt?* she asked it gently.

The hawk bounced where it perched, painlessly.

*The Singer's sent me a message!* she declared. *Let me take it!*

The hawk flew out of reach.

*Promise I won't bellow at you again,* she smiled. *Sorry, little hawk.*

The hawk sidled closer, shaking.

*Wasn't that terrible was I?* she asked, knowing as soon as she spoke that the hawk feared far worse than a shouting. Outraged on the creature's behalf she stated: *Others have tried to cage you; haven't they little hawk... Well, never me, I wish you always to be free!*

At that, a strange silver door opened inside The Knitter's heart as the hawk flew, up, up, into the rain. She watched the hawk soaring amongst the drops, blinking the wet from her eyes; drinking in rainfall, sight, and the hawk's wonderful flight.

It seemed The Singer had left her now through that doorway.

"Yendle, gone... Oh no! Was I keeping him, like The Minstrel wanted to, and the drum-makers? And is the hawk leaving too, along with The Singer's message?" she wondered, as the hawk vanished from her sight, and she was consoled only by the thought that The Singer would be back in the autumn to sing on the village green when she might speak with him again.

The hawk landed in front of her, still trembling.

*Brave little hawk.* she told it, waiting for it to be calm. But it continued to quake, and when she raised her hands eventually, slowly, to get on with untying the cloth anyway, it quaked all the more, opening its beak, on reflex, to bite.

*Please be at peace with me, this is all I have left,* she begged the hawk, bursting into tears.

But the hawk – so often mistreated by others – couldn't be calm.

Sobbing, she decided she must command it to return to its master, message undelivered, untouched, unheld, unread.

At which point, The Singer revealed he'd not left: *Test passed,* he announced in her head.

*A test?* she spoke, laughing while her tears continued to fall with the raindrops. *Well, I deserved it,* she added with a smile, sniffing.

*Yes,* The Singer replied in her mind, and, using her eyelids, now blinked the hawk to be still then blinked the hawk to close its beak, enabling her to pick at the sealing wax and ravel the slim cloth from the hawk's leg. It flew immediately away.

*Thank you!* she cried after it.

Excited, she read the message under the porch, out of the rain.

*Our house is built, our garden's stocked, and we're married, as planned. A family's to follow. I'll be singing no more on the village green. Yendle.*

She doubled in pain, like the pain the messenger had delivered to her along with the news of her parents; like the pain The Singer's father had delivered to him as a boy on piercing the unicorn's chest. And, just as the boy had then, The Knitter looked down at her own chest, fully expecting to see blood, then touched the place in amazement that there was none, then inspected her trembling hand in disbelief it wasn't red.

Within her, The Singer, disturbed, compassionate, and in pain equally, offered to help her to her feet.

*No!* she cried to the rain. *I only imagine you!*

Thunder rumbled loud, his voice inside it; booming words she couldn't all catch...

*Trust us... the wind... I feel, we feel... you know... must believe...*

"How can this be, it cannot be." she thought, collapsing upon the porch, gazing out at the storm; feeling it; hearing it; in perpetually laid bare, perpetual disbelief; his material message grasped cloth-y, waxy, in her hand.

The sun came out, showing her that, in her absence, her garden had been plundered of flowers, herbs, and fruit, and trampled upon; that her windows had been smudged with fingerprints left by prying hands; that the lock to her door had been tried. "The villagers." she thought.

She lifted the message back to her face, though knowing what it said. The words spinning.

"I'm under a spell!" she thought. "I must fight it!"

Intent on destroying the object that had misled her, she climbed to her feet, without him. She opened her front door, without him. She clambered the stairs and entered her parents' room, without him. There was the drum. Shining. She ignored it. She reached and grabbed the colourful blanket she'd knitted row by row, year on year, for the day she'd be happily married and dragged it to her tiny childhood bedroom, without him.

Sitting on her little childhood bed, using her fingers, nails, and teeth, she began to unpick the blanket with its knitted-in dreams to an unravelly thread-mountain, without him. It was while she was doing this, without him, she realised he was helping her do all these things, *without him*. As she gave into this understanding, her actions grew swifter, defter: Yendle was helping her complete this since it was what she wanted to do; speedily, so she might sleep, since rest was what she needed. Discreetly, until she'd been ready to readmit he was there and that she needed him. She couldn't help but care for him all the more deeply, even when the blanket was undone to its last stitch: a clearly hopeless heap.

*Oh why must I continue to imagine you!?* she railed, and fell asleep. She woke to the scent of amber pine and the sight of her former companion, Esther, at her bedside, wearing a glorious fresh white flower in her scrawny hair, in smooth contrast to the crone's withered old weathered old face. The mound of coloured threads had gone.

*Why did you come?* The Knitter whimpered.

*Your door was wide and the wind blew me in.* Esther replied, smiling, spooning The Knitter a hot brown liquid like soil on the tongue and elixir in the belly. *I've been with you many days. Now shush. Eat.*

As The Knitter swallowed Esther's fed spoonfuls, she thought of the wind. Wind that the thunder had commanded her to trust. What future might the wind blow her to, if, like Esther, she did trust it, she wondered? She reheard the first windblown *thud-thuddings* of Yendle's drum from years before; reheard the wind-blasts down her chimney, uncovering the drum, saving her from fire... But then his message...

*I'll be singing no more on the village green.*

She could eat no more. She turned to the wall. There she saw Yendle's face, shadowy in the contours of the plaster. She closed her eyes, only to picture him grinning in the morning sunlight, and she grinned back, helplessly, despite herself. She moaned.

*Yendle,* said Esther, matter of fact. *Now, go back to sleep.*

*What's the flower you wear in your hair?* The Knitter asked her, drowsily.

*It's who I am, showing.* Esther replied, placing her knotty hand upon her own chest. *It grows from here, inside me.*

*Are you a witch?* asked The Knitter, yawning, and she fell asleep to the sound of Esther laughing like the run of the stream beyond the hills on its way through the vale to the sea.

And so Esther nursed her. Baking, cleaning, working industriously in the house and garden while The Knitter regained her strength.

One morning, The Knitter woke weeping. Esther took her hand, her eyes bright.

*I didn't want my dream to end!* The Knitter cried, sitting bolt up. *It's a dream I've had often, only this time, different. Yendle and I were walking on grass, my hand in his, warm and solid as yours is, his hawk upon my shoulder – only it had one body, two heads – unafraid of me, to a place we'd never been with a vast lake of swans with an island of oak trees...*

*My work's done,* Esther declared. *You're well.*

*But what am I to do! How am I to live like this: always turning to face the truth, and yet, in all directions, him?* begged The Knitter. *I have it in writing, he won't be back!*

From the wooden sill beneath her east-facing window came a loud, *crack!*

*Noisy house.* explained The Knitter, sheepishly.

Esther smiled, agreeing. *Indeed it is,* reaching to the sill. *This writing?* she asked, passing Yendle's message to her from its place there, then urging her, *Read.*

*I know every word!* answered The Knitter, not meaning to, but glancing at his name, when a flash, like a sheet of lightning, lit the window-framed clear sky, brightening the room for an instant.

*Did you see that?!* squealed The Knitter, hugging her bedcovers to her neck, squeezing her knuckles against The Singer's one-pronged goatee.

*I did.* replied Esther evenly. *Like you, I see many a thing.* She brought the flower within The Knitter's reach.

The Knitter lifted her hand to touch. There was no flower to feel there, only the sparse hair at the side of Esther's old head, while the air, throughout the room, was suddenly enriched with a dark green honey fragrance. The Knitter brought her hand to her face to breathe the lingering scent.

*Esther, that's astonishing! How...*

*Shush,* replied Esther, smiling, tying her crimson shawl to her head, then turning to show The Knitter that the shawl lay flat to her scalp and the flower had vanished. *Not everything's for questioning, especially that which astonishes.*

*But...* protested The Knitter.

Esther put her finger to her lips, nodding encouragement for The Knitter to keep puzzling it out for herself. By and by, she patted The Knitter's hand stating: *It's time for me to leave.*

The Knitter raised the message to her. *But this, in sepia on cloth, is a fact, one that can't disappear!*

*Facts! Facts? Well, if you wish to talk facts...* said Esther, *it's a fact I've seen The Singer, Yendle, laying here with you in your little bed. That he's not there doesn't mean I don't see him,* Esther pointed, *or see him, his whiskers upon your chin, within you.*

The Knitter pulled the covers over her head, hotly blushing, and spoke from underneath. *Am I witch, then? Is he?*

*You wish to label us?* asked Esther. *Labels are for containers, you wish to be bottled, boxed, corked, lidded, capped, wearing a label that would earn you a ducking in the pond and a roasting if you lived? They think it's only the witches who come back up breathing when it's the witches who drown quick while they've the chance to duck out of being burnt at the stake.*

The Knitter stayed in hiding. *I don't understand!* she moaned. *How did I get to be this way?*

*Play the drum,* replied Esther.

*Join that band of merry drummers you mean?* she argued, tetchily, still buried. *I refuse to. And what would I tell my neighbours about the sound since I couldn't hardly answer interrogations about it!?* she demanded, yanking down her covers in righteous indignation.

Esther had gone.

# Chapter Five

The Knitter got up and washed and dressed considering Esther's words, still arguing. "Play, indeed! Not even Esther should make my choices for me. And, Yendle, if you wished me to play the drum, as my own, you should've told me so."

*I do,* she heard.

*Why?! Does the percussion fuel you, like logs, the fire?* she defied, descending the stairs.

Esther had left the house spotlessly tidy.

Yendle was silent. The Knitter remembered Esther warning her not everything's to be questioned, but still, she persisted as she stomped out to see how Esther had left the garden. *Does it fuel them?! Do they know your secret also?*

There came no answer.

She found the garden wall had been rebuilt taller, enclosing her herbs, flowers and fruit trees, but now curved inwards, leaving the well outside.

*How dare Esther do that!* cried The Knitter, distressed. *The well belongs 'to us'!*

*No,* soothed Yendle his heart *thud-thudding* as one with her own. *The drum.*

The Knitter placed her feet firmly upon the grassy earth, pressed her hands to the heart made so precious, with his, squeezed her eyes tight shut and whispered: *Is it my destiny to become one of your drummers, Yendle? Is that why you showed me? Is that what you truly wish of me?*

Her reply was a silvery ringing, loud, between her ears.

*Do they lay with you?* she asked, croakily.

Her answer was the image of the face of the young woman, drumming in the firelight. The Knitter imagined wearing an expression the same. *Please,* she spluttered, opening her eyes to not see it any more. *Not me, like that!*

In the grass before her lay a chip off the old wall, pale and round as a full moon. *Play the drum*, it told her.

She took slow, deliberate steps to her parents' bedroom and rested her hand on the latch for a long while without entering.

*The villagers will know*, she appealed, sighing. But still there was no rescue from her insistent calling; the silvery ringing, the light directing, the shadows arrowing, the eight-legged spider running in clockwise circles on the wall by her hesitant hand: *twist the latch, enter the room, go to the drum, and play...*

She entered. Spread on her parents' bed was her blanket, re-knitted by Esther with added colours: vivid reds and sky-blues; moonlight silvers; shadow-darks; cool greys; mud-browns; and mystical purples. She dived up onto it, her body a star-shape, and buried her face in its glorious green aromas, the softness caressing her cheeks, her nose, her lips. Then, facing the east window, she sat firmly in the middle of her new-made, remade blanket and brought the drum onto her legs where its silveriness throbbed through.

God help us...

She raised her hands, with The Singer, and, dropped them to beat the skin.

Awkward at first, she was soon *thud-thudding* rhythmically, laughing, crying, laughing again.

The very joy it was bringing forced her to cease and contemplate what she was learning. She stared towards the east in wonder, where, she now knew he was living, far, far from here. She pictured him in his workshop within the house he'd built, drum-making. He looked up into her eyes, twinkling, smiling. She twinkled and smiled back, confidently.

*I see you!* she cried as the vision faded.

Returning to the drum, she began to sing, her voice enriched with the vibration and accomplishment of his. She sang the songs of his story, the story he couldn't sing, but she knew he wished to sing. And when she finished, she had an ambition: to sing that story to him, with her own breath, to his own ears, in his sight, inviting him to learn the words, and tunes, and rhythms, and dare join in with her, alone, since she would never tell.

*Make good come of this, said the unicorn's eyes as the unicorn died...* She sat on the bed long after she'd finished playing, hugging the drum, wondering "How?"

Yendle and Esther had been right; playing it had been the best thing in the world for her to do, and if the neighbours had overheard, what of it, she thought. What concern was it of theirs if The Singer had left his drum behind, and if she chose to bang it? *To each their own*, she rehearsed, chuckling, because, hadn't her thoughts about the other drummers almost prevented her playing this, set so comfortably on top of her legs it might've been made for her?

She lay her brow upon it, rocking her head gently, gratefully, puzzling.

*To each their own...* repeated she and Yendle in singsong duet.

And slowly, smiling, she knew what she must do: cut and stitch her father's working clothes to fit her and dress in them; pack a bag with plenty food, coins, jugged water, her old knitting needles, and a skein of wool she had previously judged too plain to knit, since others might like it, she now appreciated; fold her blanket around her and belt it, sturdily; next, a coat and hat, and boots, rainproof; and under her arm, this drum, this beloved and unique drum, to set off and find the place of her dreams to which neither she nor Yendle had ever been and meet him there, wherever it may be. And, together, they would know. She kissed the drum tenderly, feeling his lips.

For it had told her by its distinct tone, at first strike, it was unlike all the others; shown her Yendle, as a young man, appalled to find, when he finally unrolled the skin to use it, that, cut by his previously inept hands, as a child, using his father's big knife, there was only enough for one. Dulled by envy and disappointment, her senses hadn't told her, on her journey, what she'd been shown again and again: that only this drum's skin shone silver like this. This...

39

*Neither you, drum, nor what's between Yendle and I, can be replicated*, she declared, then, leaving the drum in the centre of the blanket, began her preparations. By the time she was ready, it was evening. She took his cloth message and wound it around the base of the third finger of her left hand, sealing it tight with wax. *I am all your wife to me, and will be all your wife that you may wish, or none, to you*, she vowed. Then she locked her door and looked towards the place from where the sun rises, the east, where The Singer was, in his house, her heart *thud-thudding* at the thought of him there.

*Yendle, my love, I come*, she expressed blissfully, then voiced her own name: *Me, Saken, yours, I come.*

Then she turned about, by instinct, to the opposite direction and headed for the crossroads. She felt her special Yendle drop from within her. She walked on alone with faith in him that she was not deserted. When she reached the middle of the crossroads, Yendle ran back towards her, and caught the her within her by the waist and leapt them both off their feet into the air, landing them on a full moonlit path not on the compass. If a part of Yendle could leave himself while he lived out his life far away, so a part of her could leave herself while she strode unfalteringly west, with a gentle breeze at her back, trusting that their hearts would be safe together in the ether, till their reunion. The Knitter would be the name she'd use on her worldly way to meet worldly him, acceptant of what is, what was, and what was to be, determinedly hopeful that following the clues as she had since first hearing his drumbeat would bring them together when they would make good come of what had happened in the golden-leaf glade overseas.

When the villagers arrived for water the following day, the well had run dry.

*We'll have to fetch from yon stream in the vale, over them 'ills, and all through the woods, till she returns,* said one, stating the obvious.

40

# Chapter Six

Of all she met and at every place she boarded, The Knitter asked of the grassy field with the lake with the swans with the island of oak trees, yet none knew of it. She knitted tunics, shawls, and covers to keep her wool and purse stocked, and did not say from whence she came nor play anymore the drum. To any who requested this she would reply that she was keeping it for its owner until they met again. Yet before she lay her head to sleep each night she told it of her day, soft-voiced, fancying The Singer might be able to hear as the skin vibrated as if in reply. Months passed until, one evening, a landlady threw open The Knitter's door crying: *Where's the man I heard speaking with you in here, when you call yourself a spinster despite that scrap of waxy cloth on your marital finger!*

*You heard but the resonance of my prayers,* replied The Knitter. Her every word to The Singer was a prayer, her every step a prayer also.

Only after a search of the room would the landlady believe The Knitter's explanation and The Knitter left at first light, piling many extra coins than bargained on the bedside table for goodwill, wishing to avoid questioning about the incriminating drum. The landlady caught her as she was leaving by the lodging-house door.

*There's generosity!* declared the landlady, chinking her coins appreciatively. *But no goodbye?*

*Bye,* The Knitter obliged, with a smile.

*Buy?* asked the landlady, chuckling into her handful of coins. *You're a little horsey of a different colour, aren't you. Tell me, what would you be wanting with the place with the oak-wood lake?*

*To make my dreams come true,* sighed The Knitter, who had doubted many times that they ever would, or that such a place existed, and yet, each time, the presence of the drum had spurred her on, renewed in hopefulness.

The landlady stared at her, then nodded at the pure sincerity in the sound of her words, still ringing in her ears. *The place is The Palace.*

*You really didn't know did you! I thought you were trying me for loyalty to The Queen, long may she reign in God's keeping! You've seen a painting of The Royal Gardens, not knowing what it was?*

*Perhaps I have,* she replied, straining to remember if she had unwittingly been influenced by any such artwork long before her dreams had started; ruing the deficiency of her knowledge despite her travelling. Nonetheless, this was how, three days later, The Knitter came be sitting at The Palace Gate next to the driver of a hired trap, looking at the tacked-up horses tossing their heads, wondering what she would do next since the place of her dreams was locked, guarded, and high-walled, when two guards stepped forward towards her. The Knitter wondered if she was about to be seized for questioning before she had a chance to meet with Yendle and know what to do and say.

*Welcome, Saken The Knitter,* said one with a bow of her head, while the other extended his hand to help The Knitter down from the trap. *The Royal Court received word from the landlady of a lodging house of yours that you were on your way to fulfil your desire to see The Royal Gardens. Please, allow us to escort you on a tour.*

*Is Yendle The Singer here?* asked The Knitter stepping down and tying to her back a sack she had knitted for summer journeys with her purse, needles, wools, coat, blanket, and The Unicornskin Drum packed tight within it, wary that the guards' friendliness might be a trick to make her succumb to their arrest of her meek.

*No,* replied the lady guard opening a door within the gates.

Beyond, walking over the lush green grass lawns she had believed to be a field, she could see a vision of she and Yendle holding hands together approaching the distant lake, as in her dreams, and forgetting all else, she knew she must catch up with the pair and rejoin herself, body to heart at last, to be holding his hand in her very own when all would be made good. She skipped through the door into the gardens crying *Yendle!* The pair appeared not to hear her and she ran towards them faster and faster on a downward incline until she was there, the dream-her and the flesh-her united, as one, holding the hand of

– nothing – as dream-Yendle vanished; The Knitter attempted to halt; and she fell instead onto her front, face down, appreciating that only she, of the two of them, were there; accepting the guard's *No* as her nose planted into the well-kept turf like a hurled turtle under the large round bundle on her back. The hands of the guards were soon helping her up either side; the guards' voices kindly asking after her wellbeing.

*Yes, I'm unhurt,* she replied, hotly blushing, realising what a fool she was, yes indeed unhurt, beyond her feelings, and in one piece, whole; also realising that the guards' hospitableness towards her was earnest, as she admired, with them, the vast lake with its oak wood in the centre, its gliding and nesting swans, and the birds flying above in the blue sky, most likely startled by her, though not one of them Yendle's hawk.

*I wanted Yendle to be here. Am I late, was he here?*

*No,* said the gentleman guard asking her to sit down between them on the grass, and watch the swans, and talk. The guards knew much about her, they explained, or she would never have been granted permission to visit this day. Persons had been enquired of, about her, including Yendle who used to sing in her village each year, which village, the land, with its ponds, streams, farms, barns, houses, and churches, belonged to The Queen, did Saken know?

*Even my house, and the well, and the water, and the buckets?* she asked. *I was always told they belonged to us!*

*By The Queen's license, they do. You're an authorised custodian, by Her Majesty's decree,* the lady guard informed her.

The Knitter felt uncomfortable about the wall she had broken and Esther had mended with the well outside of it, and asked, *How fares Yendle?*

*Happily! His wife is with child again and he's busy with her; their firstborn; his business; and the family garden. He said he only met you twice, briefly, and found you weighed with sadness so gave you his favourite silver deerskin drum to lighten your load, and what have you done but loaded it onto your back!* said the lady guard, affably.

43

The Knitter was silent, embarrassed again. Was it really deerskin after all? And hers? Had she imagined it all? She could hardly argue without implicating him as a trespasser and witness and hider of the murder of a unicorn and herself as the gainer of knowledge by eerie means. Yet, perhaps it had only ever been a silver deerskin drum given to her in pity, and her mind had invented the rest, she feared, but then remembered how Esther had borne witness to her perceptions, yet also that Esther would not have been able to confirm this without labelling them into danger...

*Was Esther asked about me?*

*Yes, she spoke most fondly of you. Nursed you when you'd been out walking for days in foul weather and got yourself a fever, hearing and seeing impossible sounds and sights within the evident creation,* said the lady guard.

*I'm most fond of Esther too,* said The Knitter, shyly, confused about what she truly had witnessed, and what had merely been delirium, at the time of her fever, and also before it, and ever since...

*I see a face in the clouds, sometimes,* said the lady, smiling. *Of my beloved husband.*

*I was on guard last week and heard a sound that made my blood run cold, a man being murdered!* said the gentleman. *I rushed to his aid, and found it was no more than a pair of tomcats, singing!*

There was a report of trumpets and drums from behind them and the guards stood up.

*The Queen is seeing off important guests,* explained the gentleman guard. *Here's a spectacle for you! And after she has, The Queen would like to meet you, Saken.*

*Me?* asked The Knitter, standing and turning towards The Palace, her question fleeing her mind at the sight greeting her eyes. The grand doors were open onto a semicircular white stone platform with curved white steps rippling from it down to the circular forecourt where a polished black carriage with six white horses and a white-uniformed driver waited. A blood-red-uniformed band played a crisp fanfare at either corner of the platform while members of The Royal Court assembled at either side of the steps, those uniformed variously in azure, gold, and emerald, marching, those in gowns and suits gliding into place as if worked by oiled cogs, and every one sporting a fine hat. When all were at their posts The Queen and Her Royal Husband floated onto the platform with the heirs, and their guests: a couple in brightly patterned robes and brightly patterned turbans, and their attendants. The Royal Husband wore a gold coronet with three points and black clothes embossed with red details, looking to The Knitter like the king and knave of all suits of cards, whilst The Queen with her diamond crown and sweeping gown of red with white and black embossed details looked like the queen and ace of all suits.

The Knitter felt humbled by her own mannish clothing and bared head and was glad that she stood at enough distance so as not to be conspicuous. She noticed that among all these beautifully-dressed people, there was only one person – positioned at the front of a group – who was the height of a small child, full grown, whereas, in her village, there were four. She touched her own head with a shock. Five, in her own village there were five, including herself... She sat with a bump.

*What is it Saken?* asked the lady guard, crouching beside her.

*That man there, the smallest one, in the blue uniform, he's not your husband is he?*

*No,* stated the lady. *Why do you ask?*

*Would you have considered him eligible as your husband?* asked The Knitter.

*I only have eyes for my own husband,* replied the lady guard, glancing at her colleague who took her cue and crouched too.

*Is he tall, this husband your eyes are for, only?* asked The Knitter.

*He's of average stature, yet you might call him tall,* she said, with a friendly smile.

The Knitter addressed the gentleman guard: *Would a man of average stature, or tall, consider me to be an eligible wife?*

*The man you point out has a wife of a similar stature to your own,* he replied, gently. *But people of very different sizes, or shapes, or religions, or cultures, or races, or all of it, do marry sometimes.*

The gates through which The Knitter had entered via a doorway, opened, and the carriage, containing the guests, disappeared through it; The Royal Family vanished almost as one from the top of the steps; and the gathered court followed them into The Palace.

*Yendle...* whispered The Knitter in the stillness, not looking at either guard. *His wife's stature is average?*

*His wife is what even I would call tall,* stated the gentleman guard, then he shrugged, and grinned at her. *And you, so is your destiny, are what I, and most persons, would call small. Come and meet The Queen!*

The guards led The Knitter into The Palace by a lesser entrance at the side which was yet the most splendid doorway through which she had ever passed, with an ornate stone roof above its flight of steps supported by pillars carved like statues of great warriors and angels. She was led through a sparkling room the size of her village green to a long corridor with many dark closed doors along it which the guards passed with her, to halt, militaristically, before a large mirror at the very end. The Knitter hung her head at the image of herself, tiny and unkempt between the upright guards, wondering if they had brought her here for a hard look at her appearance; wondering what on earth she might do to improve it anyway, when the mirror swung outwards revealing a windowless room the size of her own cosy kitchen behind it, lit by candles in crystal-glass holders with crystal glass shades and a blazing log fire with a fat sofa in front of it, a small table set for tea in between, and The Queen, now in a long white gown embossed with pink roses with a pink band at the waist and a plain silver tiara on her head, welcoming The Knitter and dismissing the guards warmly.

Seated beside The Queen with the burden on her back removed to the side of the sofa, as bidden, The Knitter found true what she had heard rumoured, that The Queen's eyes, here glittering with light, took everything in at once. The Knitter could neither bear the penetration of

The Queen's sight, nor look away from her either: the coils of her hair which seemed they might bite; the skin of her face so delicate it seemed impertinent to view it; the prettiness of her features and form which seemed endless.

*Enjoy*, urged The Queen, passing The Knitter an empty plate with paintings of flowers so lovely, they brought a coo from The Knitter's throat like a pigeon, and gesturing with an open hand at numerous delicacies set out on a platter with the same decoration. The Knitter selected a diamond-shaped bar of marzipan pressed with The Royal Crest and spread with a fine sheet of pure gold, and accepted a steaming tea in a cup and saucer that matched the plates and the platter, poured by The Queen.

The marzipan was firm to bite then melted between her teeth before she might bite it further, and she closed her eyes to relish it, smiling, recalling the scent of Yendle, now a flavour and a texture, dissolving; the most delicious food that had ever passed her lips. She placed the plate on the table, apologising: *It is beautiful, one mouthful sufficed, more would be too much*, and sipped her tea, which refreshed her in a way she had not known a drink like tea could refresh. When the cup and saucer touched between sips, the china chinked like the dawn chorus and Saken imagined she caught the pretty scent of the painted-on flowers. After her third cup, and when The Queen had finished eating and drinking also, The Knitter glowed like the crystals, and to thank The Queen for her hospitality on this day, she humbly offered her anything at all she might possibly have to give the royal lady.

*Play your drum, and sing me a story*, stated The Queen.

*I only know one story, long and strange*, said The Knitter, frightened for Yendle and for herself as to what it might reveal, and yet, sensing that it could be safe; that this could be why she was here after all. *I've only sung it once before, to nobody but myself, and I think it might have changed since then, but I don't know what you'd make of it.*

*We shall have to see then, shan't we*, replied The Queen, expectantly.

The Knitter requested permission to put her blanket on the carpet to make herself feel at home, then took out the drum which shone starry in the candle and firelight. The Queen's eyes rounded at it, and her smile became a crescent.

*It's mainly a story I made,* said The Knitter, doubtfully, then began at an earlier beginning than she had intended, with a song about knitting her blanket, then sang on and on further than she had intended, with The Queen happily nodding her; the fire and candle flames dancing her and the rhythms of the drum *thud-thudding* her to continue; right up to a song about where they were now in the flickering room.

The Queen clapped her hands together. *How creative!*

Saken fondled her wedding finger where the cloth was tied. *It wasn't all my imagination, I did find this on the leg of Yendle's hawk, for example, though I can't be sure it was intended for me, or if even it's written in someone else's hand than his hand.*

*Yes,* The Queen affirmed, *the story is make-believe based upon what you interpreted from what you perceived to be true. Interesting. I like the part where you dreamt of The Palace Gardens, unknowingly, perhaps having seen them in a painting. I have a private painting which might interest you, which I shall show you,* she vowed, seemingly addressing the fire, then folded her hands patiently upon her lap, and waited, silently.

The Knitter took the hint that this tantalising promise could only be fulfilled after an action of her own. Guessing, she unpicked the wax and unwrapped the cloth with the writing upon it from her ring finger. She turned it to The Queen, who read it, and inspected the signature, in one glance, then looked back at the fire. The Knitter tossed the cloth into the burning logs. It landed, by chance, in a clear Y-shape, facing them, on the top of a white-ashy piece of wood, charred underneath, where there were no flames. The Knitter thought she saw a red spider of fire suspended on a thread of black smoke land upon it from down the chimney, suck it to ash, then scrabble back up in a flash. "But what do I know," she thought, miserably. "It's only what I perceive true, and no one else."

*Did you see that!* commented The Queen with flame-lit eyes. *Off like a spider!* She took The Knitter, who grinned at her, to a desk with a leather-bound folder upon it, which The Queen did not open at once. With her regal hands spread across it she said: *You may have heard tell of The Palace Gardens, if not seen a picture. Tales travel. You may have heard tell of a woman, overseas, in the land where the Yendle that we know of, was born, whose son was called Yendle, and how this her son Yendle went hunting with his father one day, against his own gentle will, and how neither returned; and how, the next morning, this Yendle's mother found her husband's bloody clothing wrapped around his bloodied knife on the doorstep and was never to see either her husband or her son again? It is a folktale.*

The Queen now opened the folder at a page marked by a decorative silver bookmark to a painting of a forest scene in winter, showing a distant castle, a circle of trees in the foreground, and within the circle, a pair of unicorns.

*The King of the foreign land where the Yendle of the folktale was born is my second cousin. This painting is by him, from a tree, so as not to startle the unicorns, and in winter, for a good view, since, in the summer months, the branches are thick with golden leaves. You must have seen a painting of this, or heard of this place, wouldn't you say, since you're no witch?*

*Must have,* The Knitter agreed, though she could not for the life of her think where or when. Her skin tingled at the sight of the unicorns, the smaller of the two in particular. *It's exactly as I conceived of it, apart from it depicting the leafless season.*

*In spite of that, are you able to recognise the precise site where you conceived of the burials within this glade, no doubt through tales you've heard told?*

The Knitter studied the trunks of the trees: *There, I think,* she replied, touching the parchment. The fire cracked and the drum resonated with the sound and both women held silence about this from one another.

"Coincidence," thought The Knitter, decisively, though her spirits sank at the loss of her hope that The Singer might be communing with her via the instrument, or communing with her in any other way at all, but she knew she must try to accept that every such hope had been misguided.

The fire cracked again, louder, and the drum gave a simultaneous *THUD!*

The Knitter gasped, and stared from The Queen, to the shining drum, to the fire, where the flames were leaping tall like a ring of golden-leafed treetops in a gale.

The Queen did not turn, but calmly spoke a prayer in a language The Knitter did not know, sighed contentedly, and closed the book saying: *Amen.*

*Amen,* said The Knitter, and the fire quelled to cheery and the drum's shine dipped. "Coincidence," she thought, purposefully.

*Of course, your drum is made of silver deerskin, we know this from the mouth of the Yendle who lives here in this land, which deer is becoming almost as rare as the unicorn. I am fond of that painting; some believe the unicorn is extinct, some do not believe it existed at all and would call this artwork fanciful.*

*What do you call it?* whispered The Knitter, flushing at a remnant hope, *thud-thudding* through her by itself, that somehow, after all this, The Queen might say something that would mean she and Yendle would at least meet again and be able to talk about what had happened, and that she would be able to check with him what she thought she had learned, and to learn from him what he had experienced, similarly, if anything...

*No living unicorn can be found and the remains of no dead unicorn can be found either. It is said by some that all the horns were ground up for magic,* The Queen laughed. *If only the Yendle known to us were the same Yendle of the folktales. I would grant him A Royal Pardon, as a child following his father's orders, and as my cherished subject, and put it to my second cousin, The King, to dig the glade, based on Yendle's sworn testimony. We do not dig up Royal Grounds based on folktales, particularly abroad, which are our relatives', with other laws, unless, in this case, we are prepared to face questions leading to accusations of witchcraft and conspiracy, whether any evidence were found or not. We let it rest in legend.*

The Queen and The Knitter returned to the sofa and both stared quietly into the quietened fire.

*What if our Yendle was the folktale Yendle, and he knew he would be spared from punishment for his father's crime?* asked The Knitter. *Might he not give testimony then?*

*Even the Yendle we know, of this land, keeps secrets: he has allowed his wife to assume he sold his favourite silver deerskin drum, before retiring from public singing, rather than giving it away, to you, another woman; and he allowed you to believe he would return for it,* The Queen informed her.

*He didn't say that,* The Knitter protested, protectively.

*He didn't tell you it was a gift, either, as he has claimed since,* The Queen asserted. *It is clear that Yendle could not give the simplest truthful testimony without unearthing some skeletal bones of his own.*

The Knitter shuddered at the idea. *I don't know if I want the drum now, come-by sly-handed. Would you like it, directly, from me?* The Knitter offered, looking at it twinkling entrancingly in the firelight, like lovers' eye-light, holding her breath waiting for The Queen's reply.

*It is yours,* said The Queen. *Yendle has said so, to my representatives, which is direct.*

The Knitter sighed, smiled, and lay her hand upon it. *It's been the source of so many of my dreams for so very long...*

*Now you know it is silver deerskin, and a kind, if covert, gift, that he will not be returning to collect, it will surely give you other dreams; dreams that can be realised,* The Queen reassured her. *If it really were unicornskin – although I feel sure you understand that you must not state this, for many reasons – you have overcome your sorrows, and passed on its story to your monarch, so good has come of the unicorn's death after all,*

51

stated The Queen. *And perhaps your feelings, and actions, were more to do with the unicorn, all along, now at peace. Take comfort and have peace also.*

*There was sorrow in Yendle too, and my heart is the drum that I gave him, what of that?* insisted The Knitter.

*Is your heart not back in your breast on finding him absent here, in The Palace Gardens, where you so hoped to meet him?* replied The Queen, firmly.

*Might he not miss it?! I hope he's overcome his sorrow,* spoke The Knitter, reflectively.

*Yendle will know the full story you told me, and my thoughts on it, individually,* The Queen told her. *And if any sorrow then remains in him, that a woman's love can mend, it will be for his wife to address. He has made his choices, you must make yours, also, individually.*

*Yes,* said The Knitter, decisively, packing away her drum, giving it a tender pat as she did so. Its tone remained beautiful, and yet, her heart no longer thud-thudded to the sound. Peace, indeed. She packed her blanket fondly around it, as her friend.

*You were fortunate to get your heart back, after giving it blindly to one who was so hungry. Care for it, with vision, Saken,* stated The Queen.

Before The Knitter had a chance to reply, The Queen had left the room and the guards had returned to lead The Knitter to a carriage which would deliver her home in safety and style. And on the way, "What am I to make of it all?" thought Saken, by herself, to the sound of the trotting horses, and the ancient well quietly refilled with water and when she arrived at it, she was able to draw upon it freely without knowing it had ever been barren until the villagers gossiped her so, pleased that the water, and she, had returned. Though it was to remain her favourite, never to be sold, or parted with, knitting her blanket had only ever been the start.

# Acknowledgements

With thanks to both my clever daughter Beatrix Bee Hamilton Crinnion, and clever friend Claire Parker, for their early, pre-submission proofreads and excellent helpful editorial suggestions.

Thanks to Angela Readman whose recommendation of Three Drops Press finally encouraged me to submit the book some three years after its completion, and for her subsequent, generous, endorsement of it.

Thanks to Dave Swann for his thoughtful endorsement too, and for his specific advice as to an aspect of punctuation. Thanks to AH for the chapter breaks idea.

Biggest thanks to Kate Garrett-Nield for falling in love with the book and painstakingly realising it in print, along with the Three Drops team, including selecting and implementing chapter divisions, final proofreading, and standardisation of details such as use and style of speech marks. Thanks to Kate also for loving and reproducing that coincidental and serendipitous photo of mine, too, for the front cover, which I took while writing the story. Pareidolia, anyone?

Thanks to my family: ex-husband Phil Crinnion, son Danie Hamilton-Coppen, Beatrix, again, and son Ted Rifky Hamilton Crinnion, for sparing me enough to do this work, yet not so much that I became quite lost to it, either.

## Other titles from Three Drops Press

*Constellations* by Susan Castillo Street
*Under-hedge Dapple* by Janet Philo
*Back to Yesterday* by Zoe Broome
*Full Moon & Foxglove: An Anthology of Witches & Witchcraft*

*Three Drops from a Cauldron: Lughnasadh 2015*
*Three Drops from a Cauldron: Samhain 2015*
*Three Drops from a Cauldron: Midwinter 2015*
*Three Drops from a Cauldron: Imbolc 2016*
*Three Drops from a Cauldron: Beltane 2016*
*Three Drops from a Cauldron: Lughnasadh 2016*
*Three Drops from a Cauldron: Samhain 2016*

### **Coming Soon**

*Tailfins & Sealskins: An Anthology of Water Lore*
*Three Drops from a Cauldron: Midwinter 2016*

*There is an island* by Johnny Giles
*Follow the Stag and Learn to Fly* by Anna Percy
*A Sprig of Rowan* by Rebecca Gethin
*The Darkling Child and Other Stories* by Catherine Blackfeather
*Among the White Roots* by Bethany W Pope
*After the Fall* by Cora Greenhill
*Lykke and the Nightbird* by A.B. Cooper
*The Princess of Vix* by Helen May Williams

www.ingramcontent.com/pod-product-compliance
Lightning Source LLC
Chambersburg PA
CBHW070810120626
46557CB00002B/797